KIDS CAN'T STOP READING THE CHOOSE YOUR OWN ADVENTURE® STORIES!

"Choose Your Own Adventure is the best thing that has come along since books themselves."

—Alysha Beyer, age 11

"I didn't read much before, but now I read my Choose Your Own Adventure books almost every night."

—Chris Brogan, age 13

"I love the control I have over what happens next."

—Kosta Efstathiou, age 17

"Choose Your Own Adventure books are so much fun to read and collect—I want them all!"

—Brendan Davin, age 11

And teachers like this series, too:

"We have read and reread, worn thin, loved, loaned, bought for others, and donated to school libraries our Choose Your Own Adventure books."

CHOOSE YOUR OWN ADVENTURE®— AND MAKE READING MORE FUN!

Bantam Books in the Choose Your Own Adventure® Series
Ask your bookseller for the books you have missed.

- #1 THE CAVE OF TIME
- #2 JOURNEY UNDER THE SEA
- #3 BY BALLOON TO THE SAHARA
- #4 SPACE AND BEYOND
- #8 DEADWOOD CITY
- #13 THE ABOMINABLE SNOWMAN
- #14 THE FORBIDDEN CASTLE
- #18 UNDERGROUND KINGDOM
- #19 SECRET OF THE PYRAMIDS
- #21 HYPERSPACE
- #22 SPACE PATROL
- #24 LOST ON THE AMAZON
- #25 PRISONER OF THE ANT PEOPLE
- #26 THE PHANTOM SUBMARINE
- #27 THE HORROR OF HIGH RIDGE
- #28 MOUNTAIN SURVIVAL
- #29 TROUBLE ON PLANET EARTH
- #31 VAMPIRE EXPRESS
- #32 TREASURE DIVER
- #33 THE DRAGON'S DEN
- #35 JOURNEY TO STONEHENGE
- #36 THE SECRET TREASURE OF TIBET
- #38 SABOTAGE
- #39 SUPERCOMPUTER
- #40 THE THRONE OF ZEUS
- #41 SEARCH FOR THE MOUNTAIN GORILLAS
- #43 GRAND CANYON ODYSSEY
- #44 THE MYSTERY OF URA SENKE
- #45 YOU ARE A SHARK
- #46 THE DEADLY SHADOW
- #47 OUTLAWS OF SHERWOOD FOREST
- #48 SPY FOR GEORGE WASHINGTON
- #49 DANGER AT ANCHOR MINE
- #50 RETURN TO THE CAVE OF TIME
- #51 THE MAGIC OF THE UNICORN
- #52 GHOST HUNTER
- #53 THE CASE OF THE SILK KING
- #54 FOREST OF FEAR
- #55 THE TRUMPET OF TERROR
- #56 THE ENCHANTED KINGDOM
- #57 THE ANTIMATTER FORMULA
- #58 STATUE OF LIBERTY ADVENTURE
- #59 TERROR ISLAND
- #60 VANISHED!
- #61 BEYOND ESCAPE!
- #62 SUGARCANE ISLAND
- #63 MYSTERY OF THE SECRET ROOM
- #64 VOLCANO!
- #65 THE MARDI GRAS MYSTERY
- #66 SECRET OF THE NINJA
- #67 SEASIDE MYSTERY
- #68 SECRET OF THE SUN GOD
- #69 ROCK AND ROLL MYSTERY
- #70 INVADERS OF THE PLANET EARTH
- #71 SPACE VAMPIRE
- #72 THE BRILLIANT DR. WOGAN
- #73 BEYOND THE GREAT WALL
- #74 LONGHORN TERRITORY
- #75 PLANET OF THE DRAGONS
- #76 THE MONA LISA IS MISSING!
- #77 THE FIRST OLYMPICS
- #78 RETURN TO ATLANTIS
- #79 MYSTERY OF THE SACRED STONES

#1 JOURNEY TO THE YEAR 3000 (A Choose Your Own Adventure Super Adventure®)
#2 DANGER ZONES (A Choose Your Own Adventure Super Adventure®)

CHOOSE YOUR OWN ADVENTURE® • 79

MYSTERY OF THE SACRED STONES

BY LOUISE MUNRO FOLEY

ILLUSTRATED BY LESLIE MORRILL

An Edward Packard Book

BANTAM BOOKS
NEW YORK • TORONTO • LONDON • SYDNEY • AUCKLAND

RL 4, Il age 10 and up

MYSTERY OF THE SACRED STONES
A Bantam Book / May 1988

CHOOSE YOUR OWN ADVENTURE® is a registered trademark of Bantam Books, a division of Bantam Doubleday Dell Publishing Group, Inc.
Registered in U.S. Patent and Trademark Office and elsewhere.

Original conception of Edward Packard
Interior art by Leslie Morrill
Cover art by James Warhola

All rights reserved.
Text copyright © 1988 by Edward Packard.
Cover art and inside illustrations copyright © 1988 by Bantam Books.
No part of this book may be reproduced or transmitted in any form or by any means, electronic or mechanical, including photocopying, recording, or by any information storage and retrieval system, without permission in writing from the publisher.
For information address: Bantam Books.

ISBN 0-553-26950-X

Published simultaneously in the United States and Canada

Bantam Books are published by Bantam Books, a division of Bantam Doubleday Dell Publishing Group, Inc. Its trademark, consisting of the words "Bantam Books" and the portrayal of a rooster, is Registered in U.S. Patent and Trademark Office and in other countries. Marca Registrada. Bantam Books, 666 Fifth Avenue, New York, New York 10103.

PRINTED IN THE UNITED STATES OF AMERICA

O 0 9 8 7 6 5 4 3

For Kris Hammargren,
with love

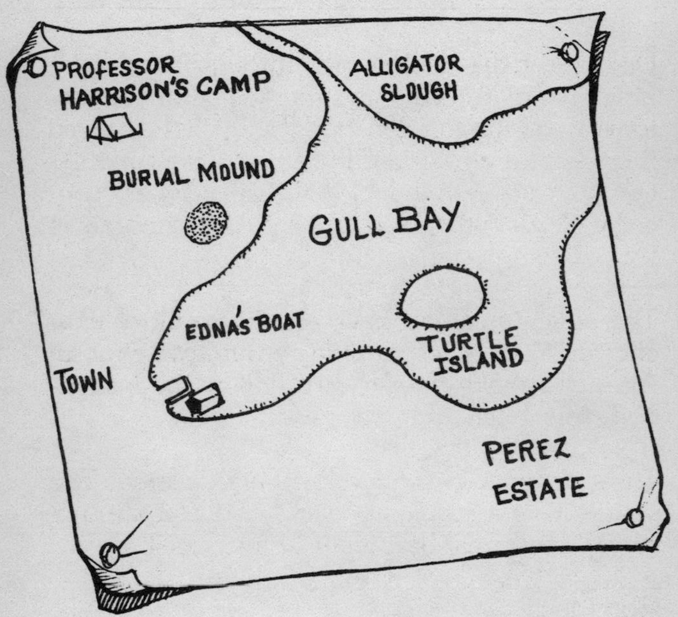
PROFESSOR HARRISON'S CAMP
ALLIGATOR SLOUGH
BURIAL MOUND
GULL BAY
EDNA'S BOAT
TURTLE ISLAND
TOWN
PEREZ ESTATE

WARNING!!!

Do not read this book straight through from beginning to end! You can have many different adventures as you try to solve the mystery of the Sacred Stones from an ancient Indian burial ground. As you read you will be able to make choices. Your choices will determine whether you succeed in solving the mystery.

The adventures you have are the result of your choices. You are responsible because *you* choose! After you make your choice, follow the instructions to see what happens to you next.

Think carefully before you make a decision. The stones have a strange power—and if you're not careful, you may be caught in their spell!

Good luck!

You're complaining to your mother about spending the summer in the city when old Mr. Canner from next door comes over to borrow a ladder.

"Where would you like to go, child?" he asks gruffly. "There's no place like home, you know."

"Home is bor-ing," you say. "It's hot, and there's nothing to do. I'd like to be anywhere but here!"

Mr. Canner chuckles and lifts his cap to scratch behind his ear. "You sound just like my sister, Edna," he says. "Got a letter from her this morning. 'Come and visit me, George,' she says. 'You must be bored daffy in the city. Bored and baked.'"

He replaces his cap and looks at you. "Course, that's not what she means at all," he continues. "She means, she wants some help paintin' and fixin' her houseboat. She broke her arm this spring. Ain't got her strength back yet."

"Houseboat!" you say. "Where does your sister live?"

"Lives in Florida. On the Gulf side."

"Are you going to go?" you ask slowly. Thoughts are spinning in your head.

"Nope, can't go till next spring. Got too many painting jobs lined up this summer. Guess I'll send her some money so she can hire someone. Edna's on a tight budget."

"Mr. Canner," you say. "I can paint and fix things. I could go and help her. For nothing." You avoid looking at your mother as you speak.

Turn to page 2.

"That's not a bad idea," says Mr. Canner. "But I don't know if you two could get along. Edna's set in her ways. Been livin' alone on that houseboat ever since her husband, Mac, died. That was twenty years ago. She's out there on the edge of a swamp. Nearest civilization is a village a mile or so away. One main street, two lampposts."

"I know I could get along with her," you say. "And I'd work hard."

"I need to talk some more with Mr. Canner," your mother says. "You go to the store and get some bread." She hands you some money.

You ride your bike to the store, wishing you were at home to hear the conversation. But you have no cause to worry: In a few days you're on a plane heading for St. Petersburg, Florida. A short, stocky woman with curly gray hair is waiting for you when you get off the plane.

"I'm Edna MacDonald," she says. "Grab your bag and let's get on the road." She leads you out to an old green pickup truck in the parking lot.

Edna talks nonstop as you drive along, telling you stories about Florida—its history, the first explorers, the wildlife, the Everglades. You scarcely realize that two hours have passed until you notice the sun is setting.

"We're almost there," she says.

"You know a lot about the state," you say as she steers onto a narrow road bordered on both sides by tropical greenery. It's barely more than a trail.

Edna nods. "I've lived here for forty years," she says. "Came as a bride and never left."

Turn to page 8.

"No need to get upset, Mrs. MacDonald," the man says, fingering the expensive camera hanging around his neck. "I haven't disturbed anything. I just wanted to get a better angle of the sunset. The roof of your cabin provided me with the perfect view."

"How do you know my name?" Edna demands.

He doesn't answer but jumps lightly to the pier. You realize that he'll have to pass you to get to his Jeep and brace yourself to stop him. But to your surprise he turns and walks the other way—down the length of the pier, toward the water. As he reaches the end you hear the sound of a boat motor starting up. He's not alone. Someone is waiting for him under the pier!

At the same time an engine crackles to life behind you. You whirl around. Someone is starting up the Jeep!

If you run to get the Jeep's license number,
turn to page 11.

If you head for the end of the pier,
turn to page 32.

"Many tribes had a concept that a few particular individuals were so thoroughly wicked that no time frame would claim them. They were called Evil Ancients, and it was believed that they floated back and forth through time, causing destruction in order to satisfy their own desires."

"That's spooky," you say, not quite believing, yet knowing that something supernatural has happened. "How did we get here? And where are we? And what's the experiment she's talking about?"

"I don't have answers for all of those questions," the professor says. "When she brought me in, we came through a room filled with artifacts from many tribes and civilizations. I recognized some of them. She wanted the Calusa Gull Rocks to add to her collection. It's my guess that she's going to test their magic powers, using us as guinea pigs."

"She's already tested one power," Edna says indignantly. "I was walking along, right as rain, and whammo! Suddenly I was on the ground, paralyzed. Like a mummy!"

"Exactly like a mummy," says Professor Harrison. "She was practicing an ancient Egyptian art that extracts the will and leaves only a shell—the body."

"Where are we?" you ask the professor in a frightened voice.

"Somewhere between time frames, I would guess," he says. "In a place that doesn't exist for the real world. We're in a space that Aphir has created in order to work her evil and only nature's forces can stop her."

Turn to page 65.

You turn and run back toward the boat. The light in the *Jolly Mac*'s cabin is comforting. You hear the mournful cry of gulls as you jump to the deck, and you look up. Three gulls are circling close over the boat. You wrench open the cabin door. The place has been ransacked! A small chest by the easy chair in the cabin has been opened and the contents strewn about, and Edna's bedroom is cluttered with clothing thrown from her bureau drawers.

The sound of the gulls gets louder. You move to the two-way radio sitting on the counter and turn on the transmitter. That's when you notice that the rock with the gull etching is gone! You hear a noise behind you and whirl around.

Turn to page 14.

"Wait till Matthew hears about this!" Edna says as she drives along the bumpy trail to the village. "He's been working with a conservation group to get the island declared a sanctuary. They were trying to get the turtles to come back. Maybe it worked!"

The main street is deserted except for a few parked cars. The stores are closed, and there's not a person in sight. Edna wheels the truck up a narrow lane between two stores and into a back alley. A sign on the building says NICHOLLS' DRUGSTORE. Upstairs, over the store, you see a light shining through some venetian blinds.

"That's Matthew's office," Edna says, pointing to the window.

At the top of a flight of wooden stairs a door is open. You follow Edna inside. A young woman is seated at a desk.

"Where's Matt?" Edna asks.

The woman stands up as you stare at her in disbelief. It's the woman from the island! Only now she's dressed in a ranger's uniform, and there's a revolver in a holster on her belt. She looks carefully at both of you and then speaks.

"I'm Julie Loomis. Matthew's on vacation this week. I'm temporarily assigned to this station. Can I help you?"

"I suppose you can," Edna says, "if Matt's not available. Somebody's got to save those turtles."

Julie's eyebrows raise just a fraction. "Turtles?"

Turn to page 56.

GIVE A
DON'T
POLLUTE

"What happened to your husband?" you ask hesitantly.

"Mac?" she says softly. "He was out on the Gulf when a storm came up. They never found him or his boat."

"That's terrible," you say.

"Yes," she replies. "It was. That was twenty years ago."

She veers to the left into a clearing, and points at a gray, weatherworn houseboat tied up alongside a rickety pier. "Here we are. That's the *Jolly Mac*!"

"Who's that man on the cabin roof taking pictures?" you ask. "I thought you lived alone."

"I do," Edna says grimly, slamming on the brakes. She jumps out.

"That must be his red Jeep parked over there!" you yell as you run to catch up with her.

Edna glances over her shoulder at the vehicle. "Never saw it before in my life," she snaps. "Him either."

"Hey!" she yells at the man. "You're trespassing. Get off my boat!" She hits the pier on the run, with you right behind.

The man is big and blond. He has the muscular build of a bodybuilder. He turns at the sound of her voice. Instinctively you know you don't like him. His white shorts and shirt show off a beautiful tan, but his gray eyes are cold, even though he smiles as Edna approaches. You reach down and pick up a piece of wood from the pier—just in case.

Turn to page 3.

When you get back to the boat, Edna heats some chowder while you make up a bed for yourself on the sofa. You notice that several times she glances at the rock on the drainboard, and you wonder what is so special about it. But you're too tired to ask. When you've finished eating, you both turn in for the night.

"Have a good sleep," Edna says, pausing at the door to her bedroom. "The couch is pretty comfortable, and in a few days you'll get used to the motion of the boat and the sound of the water."

"I won't hear a thing," you tell her, biting back a yawn.

But you're wrong. You don't know what time it is when you wake up, but you sense the presence of another person in the cabin. You open your eyes just a slit and lie very still. Someone with a flashlight is searching the room. The moonlight beams in through the window, and you get a glimpse of the person's face. It's the driver of the Jeep! She has the flashlight trained on the drainboard, and you watch as she picks up the rock and silently leaves. Should you follow the intruder? Or get Edna?

If you follow the intruder, turn to page 46.

If you wake up Edna, turn to page 108.

You run toward the Jeep. You know it can't get out of the clearing quickly. The road is too rough and too narrow.

The driver, a dark-haired woman, sees you coming and steps on the gas. The motor floods, dies, and then starts up again. A younger woman hurries from the underbrush. She stoops to pick up something, sees you, and instead, runs for the Jeep.

"Stop!" you yell as she leaps into the passenger seat.

The Jeep bounces out of the clearing, but not before you notice that the license-plate frame is empty, and that a large scratch mars the shiny red finish on the driver's side.

Disappointed, you walk over to see what the woman left behind. There are some pretty shells, some brown-and-black objects that look like teeth, and a strange slab of rock with unusual markings on the top. The jagged edge along one side tells you that it has been broken off a larger piece.

"They got away," you tell Edna when you get back to the houseboat. "But they left these. What are they? They look like teeth."

"That's exactly what they are," she says. "Fossilized sharks' teeth. There are thousands up and down the coast."

You hand her the rock. "They left this too."

Edna draws in a quick breath. "From a burial mound," she whispers. Her hands tremble slightly as she examines the markings, and she sets it down carefully on the drainboard.

Turn to page 37.

"I don't remember anything about the woman," you say.

Julie slams the clipboard down on the desk. "Nothing?" she asks pointedly.

"Nothing," you say. "She wasn't as close to me as the man."

"Not if she was fat or thin or short or tall?" Julie asks.

You shake your head. Your hands feel clammy, and your throat is tight.

Julie looks at her watch and stands up. "There's still time," she says. "Let's go."

"Where?" you ask, dreading her answer.

"Where do you think, child?" asks Edna, as if you were a dunce. "To Turtle Island."

Your heart sinks. If Julie gets you and Edna to Turtle Island, she and the man could kill you both. Your bodies would be dumped out to sea, and nobody would ever know what happened.

Turn to page 22.

"I'll stay in the boat and keep watch," you tell Edna.

"Good," she replies. "We need to agree on a signal to warn each other. One whistle will mean I've spotted them, and I'm coming back to the boat. Two whistles will mean that you should get the boat out of sight. Row farther into the slough. I'll hide on the barge."

"I'm not going to go and leave you on the barge!" you insist.

"Do what I say," she tells you. "When the coast is clear, I'll whistle three times. Then come back and get me."

Turn to page 30.

The driver of the Jeep is standing in the doorway. She is wearing a long shimmering white dress that reminds you of the burial mound. Her headdress reminds you of pictures you've seen of an Egyptian princess. A white gull sits motionless on her shoulder, and in her outstretched hands she holds the rock you brought to Edna—*and its mate*!

"Who are you?" you demand. "What have you done with Edna?"

"I have come from another time and place," she says in a heavily accented voice, "to retrieve what belongs to my people. The woman Edna had what was not hers. She has paid the price—and so will you!"

"Don't threaten me!" you say, whirling around to face the radio. You grab the microphone. "Mayday! Mayday! This is the *Jolly Mac*!"

As you speak the gull dives from her shoulder. You cover your head with your arm and feel a stinging pain in your hand.

Turn to page 36.

You enter the cabin first, and find yourself facing a gun. The woman from the Jeep grabs your arm and pulls you in front of her, pressing the gun into your back.

"The rock, Mrs. MacDonald," she says to Edna. "Give me the rock, or your young friend gets shot. I know you have the mate."

Edna doesn't hesitate. She walks to a small chest and searches through its contents. With a sigh she pulls out the ancient treasure—the mate to the Calusa Gull Rock!

The woman's eyes show a flash of excitement. "Now, both of you get into the bedroom," she orders, pushing you.

Your temper flares. "You stole the wrong one!" you say. "You'll never get the mate."

"But you are wrong," she replies. "I relieved Dr. Harrison's assistant of the other stone this morning. He is on his way to Miami with the decoy I stole from here last night!"

You wrench free of her grasp. "How did you know about the student assistant going to Miami?" you ask.

"I occupy the tent next to Professor Harrison's," she says, smiling. "I overheard your conversation this morning."

Go on to the next page.

"You're on Harry's dig team?" Edna asks.

"I'm a visiting professor from Egypt," she replies, "with a specialty in shamanism and sacred artifacts. Having the Calusa Gull Rocks in our permanent collection will be a coup!"

She waves the gun at you. "Into the bedroom!"

"You'll never get away with it!" you yell through the door as she barricades it from the outside. "The state police will catch you before you go ten miles. They'll set up roadblocks!"

Turn to page 23.

"I can wait to eat," you tell Edna. "Let's drive over there if it will make you feel better."

"There are no roads in there, child!" she says. "We'll take the boat. But you'll have to row. My bad arm is too weak to row that distance. Run and get the lanterns from the cabin!"

You do as she says and follow her into a small boat docked beneath the pier. "Who owns Alligator Slough?" you ask.

"The State of Florida," Edna answers. "It's a wildlife sanctuary, and there's a mangrove forest behind the beach area and a sizable population of brown pelicans. I just don't understand it."

The oars dip quietly in and out of the water as you head north. "What will you do if the men *are* there?" you ask her.

"Nothing," says Edna. "We'll just observe and report to the ranger station in the morning." She holds up her lantern and peers through the darkness. "Head for the shore. We're close to the mouth of the slough."

You propel the boat toward a lagoon on the shoreline. Dense foliage comes down to the water's edge at the entrance, and the moon, playing on remnants of dead mangrove trees, throws grotesque shadows on the water. You watch warily for alligators and water snakes.

"It's spooky in here," you say to Edna.

She holds up her hand to silence you, and you look to where she is looking. Amid nature's primitive jungle you see the hulking silhouettes of modern machinery.

Turn to page 42.

"I'll go to the *Jolly Mac,*" you say quickly, thinking about the eerily beautiful burial site.

The professor nods. "Good. Be careful." He pulls into the clearing and parks the Jeep. You tell him how to reach the burial mound and then head for the boat.

You approach the *Jolly Mac* with caution. A light shows through the curtains on the cabin window, and you try to remember if you and Edna left one burning. You jump lightly onto the deck and enter. Edna's oil lantern is on the counter, casting a warm yellow glow through the room. The rock you picked up in the clearing is beside it. Nothing appears to be disturbed.

The small chest that the professor described is in a corner behind a chair. You kneel in front of it, lifting the wooden lid to expose an assortment of things—letters, a snapshot album, an old quilt. Your fingers grope through its depths until your hand rests on something hard The rock! Carefully you lift it out and look at it. You are about to get up and match it up with the one on the counter when you sense that someone else is in the room. Slowly you turn. Aphir is standing by the counter, holding the mate to the rock in your hand.

"Give it to me," she says, staring into your eyes.

You feel paralyzed. Is it fear? you wonder. Or is she casting a spell on you as she did on Dr. Colby?

The flame from the oil lamp flickers slightly as a breeze moves the curtains at the window.

"Give it to me," she repeats, approaching you slowly.

Turn to page 106.

"I'd like to explore Gull Bay," you tell Edna.

She points to a rowboat under the pier. "There's your transportation. It's old but sturdy. Put on a life jacket, and take the binoculars. You may want to do some bird-watching."

The oars are awkward at first, but once you get into a rhythm, the boat glides along smoothly. A half-moon of white beach rims a small cove north of the *Jolly Mac,* and offshore there is a small island. You decide to stop at the island and look for whales' teeth. You tie the boat to a short dock and walk along the sand, picking up shells as you go. Just as you're about to head back to the boat, you hear voices. You move to the shelter of some low foliage. Farther down the beach a man and woman are filling pails with something. Are they clamming? you wonder. You lift the binoculars and step out of the foliage. That was a mistake, you tell yourself. The man looks up.

"Hey! What are you doing here?" he yells, running toward you.

Turn to page 62.

Julie hustles you and Edna downstairs and into her Jeep, and you ride in silence to the pier north of town, where the ranger's launch is docked. It's the biggest and most powerful boat you've ever seen. Within minutes the three of you are aboard the launch, skimming across the open water, headed for Turtle Island. If her partner is still there, you and Edna will be no match for them. Julie activates the two-way radio and speaks into the microphone. You can't hear what she says. Maybe she's warning the man! you tell yourself. She turns and looks at you.

"Letting the main office know what I'm up to," she explains.

"What if he picks up your signal on the island?" you ask.

"He?" she says, frowning. "Nothing can outrun this boat."

"They," you reply, wishing you hadn't said anything.

Turn to page 73.

You hear the woman laugh. "Yes, they will look for me on the roads, but I will be in the skies!" As she speaks you hear the loud throbbing of an engine. You rush to the tiny window. Sitting on floats in the water is a small white plane. You turn to Edna. She is pale and shaking.

"Hurry!" you say, pushing on the door. "Let's get out of here!"

Edna shakes her head. "There's no hurry," she says, her voice quivering. "She is doomed. She does not respect the power of the rocks. She will never get them back to her country."

"That's silly superstition," you say. "The rocks don't have any power!"

By the time you push through the barricaded door, the seaplane is taxiing across the bay.

"Radio someone!" you say to Edna. "Warn them!"

"She's taken the tubes," Edna says, examining the radio. "The set is inoperative. We'll have to drive to the village."

Turn to page 110.

After breakfast the next day Edna hands you a wire brush. "Scrape the old paint off the pier," she says. "That'll keep you out of trouble!"

You sigh. The pier looks as though it's a mile long.

"I'll be back as soon as I can," she says.

"Aren't you going to take the rock with you?" you ask.

Edna shakes her head. "It's safer in the refrigerator than it is in the truck with me. That woman, whoever she is, is going to watch my every move."

When the truck has disappeared down the trail, you go back into the boat and straight to the chest. It's full of interesting things: a bundle of letters to Mac from the university, fishing gear, a compass, hip boots, and a heavy raincoat and hat. You're about to give up when your fingers feel something hard—rock-hard—down under the rain gear. It's the other half of the sacred rock!

You run to the refrigerator to get its mate and carefully line them up, side by side. The broken edges match perfectly! You squat down and look at the gull. The primitive beauty of the rocks fascinates you, but do they really hold special powers? you wonder. You doubt it—but there's only one way to find out for certain. Do you dare? Maybe you should wait until Edna gets back with Professor Harrison.

If you decide to test the power of the rocks, turn to page 58.

If you decide to wait, turn to page 115.

Edna talks into the mike, and you open the door a crack so you can watch for the men. You hear her mention Alligator Slough and titanium.

"Edna, they're coming down the stairs!" you say.

Just as she puts down the mike, the barge shudders. Someone has turned on the generator. The door opens, and the room is flooded with light.

"Good evening, Mrs. MacDonald," says the man who was on the *Jolly Mac*. "I'm sorry you had to go snooping, although I expected it. Now we'll have to take you both for a ride. Your last ride," he adds pointedly.

"What do you plan to do with us, Mr. Randall?" Edna demands.

"Oh, we'll drop you in the Gulf, about halfway to Texas."

Edna snorts. "That little motorboat of yours doesn't hold enough fuel to get up to Tampa," she says.

"We're not taking the motorboat," Randall replies. As he speaks the barge lurches, and you hear a gushing sound. "Once the sand is emptied—that's what Jake is doing now—we will be underway."

Go on to the next page.

"In a barge?" you ask. "Barges have to be pulled or pushed."

"Many do," he agrees. "But this barge has a high-powered diesel engine. It's self-propelled."

"Why are you dumping the sand?" you ask him, stalling for time. "Getting rid of the evidence?"

"Not at all," he replies. "For every load we take out, we bring one in. Otherwise the nature of the coastline would change, and someone might become suspicious."

Turn to page 111.

You walk along the hallway toward the stairs, your sneakers squeaking on the metal floor. You're just a few steps behind Edna and Randall. Edna looks back at you and winks. She must suspect you're planning something.

They start up the open staircase, but you stop on the bottom step. They've almost reached the top when Randall turns around. When he does, Edna catches him off-balance and gives him a shove. You jump aside. He lets out a yell as he topples backward down the stairs, hitting his head on the bottom step. His gun clatters and skids as it hits the metal floor.

"I'll get the gun! You go to the engine room!" Edna shouts.

You rush into the small hot room. Jake is not there. You start shutting things down. One by one the motors cut out until the boat is still and silent. You hear a yell and footsteps on the stairs. A shot! You dash into the hallway.

Edna is standing at the foot of the stairs with the gun trained on Jake.

"Come down those stairs slowly," she tells him. "I'm an expert shot. You just sit down there by your sleeping friend. And don't move."

Turn to page 67.

With that Edna picks up one of the lanterns and starts climbing the ladder to the barge. When she is over the side and into the larger boat, you position yourself to watch the mouth of the slough.

Many thoughts spin through your head. What if there's another entrance to the area? What if someone comes in on the other side of the barge? Why was the man taking pictures of Alligator Slough from the *Jolly Mac*? Is there really titanium in the sand? Something glides through the water beside you, and you shiver. A water snake? An alligator? From somewhere beyond the fringes of the tropical forest a bird or an animal shrieks out. Your stomach rumbles, and you realize you're hungry—and afraid.

Suddenly from the barge comes the sound of a whistle. A second whistle! Should you go off and leave Edna? Or should you go aboard the barge and help her?

If you row deeper into the slough,
turn to page 76.

If you board the barge to help Edna,
turn to page 96.

"To Officer Porter's apartment!" you yell. "And hurry!"

Furious, the woman snatches the receiver from your hand and slams it down on the cradle.

"You'll regret that," she says, staring into your eyes.

You try to look away but find it's impossible to break eye contact. You feel your strength draining away, and you crumple to the floor.

The last thing you hear is the phone ringing. The woman does not answer it. The last thing you think is that the operator is trying to verify the emergency call.

When the ambulance arrives, it is too late for either you or Officer Porter.

Turn to page 103.

You race down the length of the pier, reaching the end just as the man jumps into the boat.

He turns and waves insolently as the driver steers the boat out into the Gulf. You notice that a telescope, a computer console, and a metal case are mounted in the rear of the craft.

"They sure don't look like ordinary tourists," Edna mutters after she joins you, watching until the boat is out of sight. "I wonder who they are."

"And I wonder what he was taking pictures of," you add.

"Let's reenact the scene," Edna says. She walks back to her boat and climbs the ladder to the sun deck to position herself in the same place the man was standing. "Sunset, my foot!" she says. "He was facing northeast, to the left of my telescope."

She looks through the instrument mounted on the roof. "Take a look," she says, moving over. "And tell me what you see."

"Just a stretch of shoreline and a bunch of trees," you reply. "It's pretty dark to see much of anything."

Go on to the next page.

"That's Alligator Slough," she says. "I haven't been there in years. Nobody goes there. Can't imagine what his interest would be."

"Are there really alligators there?" you ask.

"You betcha!" Edna says. "Lots of them. Mean critters."

"Maybe he just wanted pictures of the shoreline." you say.

"He could have taken those from his boat," Edna snaps. "Maybe we should run over to the slough." She looks at you questioningly. "If you're not too tired and hungry. I'm really curious about that fellow."

You are hungry, and tired too. Why do the man's actions trouble her so? you wonder. He was trespassing, but he seemed harmless.

If you agree to go to Alligator Slough now,
turn to page 19.

If you talk Edna into waiting until morning,
turn to page 63.

You tighten your fingers around the rock. Lightning flashes through the room. You raise your arm to throw, but you lack the strength to hurl it. With a feeble thump it lands on the floor near Aphir.

"Resistance is useless," she says, sneering at you. "You do not have the power to thwart my control." She picks up the rock and places it beside its mate. "Now, come here." She stretches out her hands to you.

You must resist her! you tell yourself. You jam your hands into your pockets and hold your ground, unmoving. Rain pounds down, and thunder vibrates the glass room. Your fingers curl around the clam shell that the professor gave you. It feels warm to your touch and seems to pulsate in your hand. Slowly you draw it from your pocket. You start moving toward her.

"Stop!" Aphir commands. "What is in your hand? Give it to me!" She snatches the shell from you, and as she does her face distorts with pain. Aphir screams and falls to the floor.

Suddenly glass is flying all around you. The ceiling and walls of the room collapse, and you throw your arms over your head and duck under a large bush for protection. The storm rages. Plants topple, and rain sweeps through the room. You crawl through the broken glass to the place where Aphir has fallen. She lies motionless on top of the Calusa Rocks, with a shard of glass imbedded in her throat. Your clam shell lies on the floor beside her. You pick it up. As you do, you're aware of voices around you.

Turn to page 118.

You cry out and grab a towel from the sink, slapping it at the bird like a whip. But now the cabin is filled with gulls diving at you, striking you with their beaks. You feel the *Jolly Mac* moving and rush to a window, protecting yourself from the attacking birds as best you can.

The deck and the hull are covered with gulls, beating their wings in an eerie rhythm that builds in power and sound. The boat is moving out into the Gulf. The birds outside are propelling it to the open water by sheer wing power!

"You can't do this!" you scream, turning to face the woman.

But she only smiles as she backs out through the cabin door. The gulls follow her, and she closes the door firmly.

You run back to the radio, trying to ignore the painful wounds on your head and hands and arms. But the radio is dead, and the boat is now ominously still. Terrified, you creep to a window. The woman is gone. The first light of dawn hangs over the water as wave after wave of gulls glide to a resting place on the *Jolly Mac.* Hundreds of birds! Thousands! Layer on layer of silent gulls, weighing the boat down. Slowly it begins to sink.

Turn to page 59.

"The etching looks like a bird," you say, "but the rock is broken. We have only a piece of it."

Edna nods excitedly. "Yes, the rock has a mate. Come and show me where the woman came out of the underbrush—and hurry! We don't have much light left." She goes to her bedroom and brings you a flannel shirt. "Put this on to protect your arms. The marsh grass will cut." She grabs a flashlight and hands you a lantern, and you hurry to the clearing.

"This is where she came out," you say, pushing through the foliage. "Can you tell me what we're looking for?"

"Yes, child," Edna says. "We're looking for the Gull Bay burial mound of the Calusa Indians."

"Burial mound," you say, with a shiver.

Edna nods. "The Calusas lived in Florida hundreds of years ago. Before the Seminoles. There is a legend that part of the tribe was sent to this area to protect the land from explorers. The Spaniards had already come in up North. It's said they settled at Gull Bay, but no one has ever been able to find their burial mound. That's one reason Mac bought this land. He was certain the burial site was close."

"Was Mac an archaeologist?" you ask.

"No, he was a fisherman. But he knew more about Florida's history than most of the archaeology professors at the university. He grew up on the Gulf. Professor Harrison even used to have Mac talk to his classes and show them his collection of artifacts. Harry Harrison is working on a dig east of the village this summer."

Turn to page 99.

"Where are you?" Professor Harrison calls out.

You try to warn him away, but no sound comes from your throat. You try to move, but you're paralyzed! As he comes closer you see that he is carrying the precious Gull Rocks, one in each hand.

"Thank you, Professor," Aphir says. "How nice of you to bring the rocks. I knew that was what you were searching for on the boat. That's why I didn't interrupt you."

"Why do you want them, Aphir?" the professor asks.

The woman's eyes are gleaming. "With the rocks," she says, "I will be able to control nature. To make myself into a gull will give me power beyond the natural elements! Then nothing can destroy me!"

"Don't use them for personal gain, Aphir," the professor warns. "We don't know their full power." His voice is strained and his eyes look glassy. He tries to look away from her but can't. He's falling under her spell!

"Give them to me," she demands.

He hesitates and then, in a trance, hands Aphir the rocks.

"Thank you, Professor," Aphir says. "Now I want you to walk backward very slowly. The earth is ready to receive you."

Go on to the next page.

Obediently the professor starts walking backward. He takes a few steps, and then suddenly he is no longer able to lift his feet. He's mired in one of the quicksand pockets that Edna warned you about!

"The more you struggle," Aphir says, smiling, "the faster you will sink. And if you sink too quickly, you will not see the power of the stones at work." She looks over at you. "Our young friend here is going to demonstrate that for us."

You're terrified! She's going to change you into a gull!

Turn to page 48.

You decide to go with Edna and Randall. Jake meets you on the top deck.

"All set," he says. "I've dropped the sand."

"Go down and start it up," Randall orders. "Mrs. MacDonald thought we were leaving in the motorboat. That's why she radioed her fisherman friend. Told him to bring a ranger." He laughs nastily. "Roll right over them if you have to."

"Right," says Jake, going downstairs.

You feel the barge lurch and move forward. Randall forces you to the deck side facing the Gulf.

"I want you two to be very visible," he says.

As your craft approaches Alligator Slough you see a small fishing boat with a spotlight trained on the barge. That must be Albert! The barge keeps moving. They're going to run right over him!

Suddenly, one by one, lights start going on all over the bay. For as far as you can see, the water is covered with boats, each one with its headlight focused on the barge.

Randall lets go of your arm. The barge motor chokes and dies. You whirl around. Behind you is a man in a ranger's uniform. He has Randall in custody and is snapping on the handcuffs!

"Evening, Mrs. Mac," says the ranger. "Albert and I came in by a canal from the east." He nods toward the fleet out in the bay. "The rest of the fellows who picked up the message came by the Gulf. You sure do have a lot of friends."

Tears glisten in Edna's eyes. "I sure do, Matt," she says, giving you a hug. "And I'm grateful to all of them. The old and the new."

The End

Two metal barges sit low in the water ahead, one with a scoop shovel mounted onto its flat surface, the other bearing a load of sand. Signs of dredging are apparent on the beach area.

"I don't get it," you say to Edna as you emerge from the entrance of the slough into a small pocket cove. "What's going on?"

"I'm not sure," she replies slowly. "But the dredging equipment makes me think that they might be after titanium."

"Titanium?" you repeat.

"Yes. Mac told me years ago that the sand around Alligator Slough was rich in titanium, but when developers tried to lease the land, the state smelled a rat and declared the area a sanctuary. Let's get in closer."

You row alongside the barge loaded with sand. A metal ladder hangs from its side.

"We could go aboard and take a look," you say.

"Yes," Edna agrees. "But one of us must stay with the boat and keep watch. Just in case someone should come." She reaches over and touches your arm. "Whatever is being done here is illegal, child," she continues. "We could be in for a lot of trouble. But now that we're here, we're here. Which would you rather do? Keep watch in the boat, or go aboard the barge?"

If you choose to stay in the rowboat, turn to page 13.

If you go aboard the barge, turn to page 68.

Without a second thought you leap off the pier at the departing rowboat. But you misjudge the distance by a fraction.

You can hear your ankle crack as one foot hits the rim of the boat, while the rest of you lands in the water. With searing pain traveling up your leg and into your thigh, you watch helplessly as the boat glides away, the oars making a rhythmic sound as they cut the water.

Using your arms and your one good leg, you propel yourself over to the nearest piling and call for Edna.

She takes you to the doctor in the village, and your broken ankle is put in a cast. Later that week you're put on a plane for home.

All you have to show for your Florida vacation is a few fossilized sharks' teeth and a handful of pretty shells.

You spend a hot summer in the city, but it's not as boring as you expected. You collect a lot of autographs on your cast, tell some tall tales about your houseboat adventure, and—at Edna's invitation—you start making plans to spend next summer on the *Jolly Mac.*

The End

Your body and tongue are paralyzed by fear.

"I will volunteer," says the professor, walking toward her. At the door he turns to face you and Edna. "I'll return," he promises reassuringly.

The door closes behind them, and you and Edna sit in silence, unable even to imagine what is happening to Professor Harrison. Your hand opens and closes around the clam shell, and you hope against hope that it will work some kind of magic to save you.

You're lost in your own terrifying thoughts when the door opens again. Aphir stands there, smiling.

"Who will be next?" she asks.

"I will," you say, clasping your clam shell tightly. You can't stand waiting any longer.

You walk to the door, and she motions for you to precede her. As she does you hear a soft whir of wings, and a sea gull glides down the hallway and into the room. In its mouth it holds a clam shell.

The professor has kept his promise to return.

"Come," Aphir says impatiently.

You know the fate that awaits you.

The End

"I don't get it," you say as Edna grabs the truck keys. "Why do you think the turtles are back? And why are we going to the village?"

"Because," she replies, "I think those 'Ping-Pong balls' you saw were turtle eggs. And the couple you saw are poachers. What I don't understand is why the ranger's patrol boat didn't see them. Matt usually makes an afternoon run."

"No wonder they were so upset when they saw me," you say.

"They'll have some stiff fines to pay if I have my way!"

"Can't you use the radio to call the ranger?" you ask.

Edna shakes her head. "That pair will have a receiver on their boat. I don't want to give them any warning. Depending on how many nests there are, they may still be there. Let's go upstairs and take a look."

You follow her outside and up the ladder to the roof of the cabin, and Edna adjusts the telescope and looks in the direction of the island.

"Do you see them?" you ask.

"I see the man," she says, motioning for you to look. "Their boat must be on the north side."

"I didn't see a boat at all," you tell her. "But then, I left in a hurry."

"Come on!" Edna cries. "We're going to town!"

She goes down the ladder, grabs her purse from the cabin, and heads for the truck in the clearing.

Turn to page 6.

You swing your legs over the side of the couch and hurry after the woman.

She walks quickly toward the water end of the pier, turning once to look over her shoulder. She sees you! Your feet slam down hard on the weathered boards of the dock as you race after her. You're gaining! In the soft moonlight you see her reach for something at her waist. You throw yourself down flat on the pier as a knife flashes through the air and embeds itself in a piling behind you.

She drops to a waiting rowboat, and a light goes on in Edna's room. She must have heard the running. But you can't wait for Edna. The woman's going to escape if you don't do something! Just a few feet away is the board you picked up this afternoon to defend yourself. She can't get away quickly in a rowboat. If your aim is good, you ought to be able to stun her. Or you could leap into the boat with her!

If you decide to throw the board, turn to page 101.

If you leap into the rowboat, turn to page 43.

Aphir moves in front of you and places the rocks at your feet.

"Step on them," she orders.

When she speaks, the lone gull that was hovering over the burial mound zooms down and lands on the ground near you. As your foot touches the rock the sea gull hops around to face you.

"Now the other foot," Aphir says coldly.

You step on the other rock, and suddenly the quiet of dawn is filled with an ominous hum. You feel your strength returning. You look up. Thousands of gulls fill the sky overhead.

"Run!" yells Professor Harrison.

You race for the marsh grass and fling yourself down beside Edna, who has suddenly returned to normal and is sitting up, watching the spectacle.

"She's a goner," says Edna quietly. "Her power is gone."

Turn to page 117.

"I'll take the path to the North," you tell Edna.

"Hold the lantern high, and watch where you step," she warns.

"Are there wild animals out here?" you ask. "Or snakes?"

"Yup, to both. But they won't bother you if they see your light. And watch out for pockets of quicksand."

"Quicksand!" you repeat.

"We won't go in far tonight," she continues, checking her watch. "I'll meet you back here in fifteen minutes."

You nod and start off through the grass, with the lantern held above your head. You can hear the Gulf waters lapping at the shore, and once in a while a night bird calls out. You wish you'd asked Edna what a burial mound looked like. What if you don't recognize it?

Turn to page 55.

"Officer Porter," you say, watching his open eyes. His body remains still, but you see a flicker of recognition when you say his name. You put your hand on his wrist. His pulse is faint, but he is not dead. "I'll get a doctor," you say, backing away.

Your mind is racing. Two cases of paralysis in one night? Edna's words haunt you. "The Calusa witchcraft is powerful!" But you don't believe in witchcraft! It must be coincidence. A flash of lightning makes you jump.

There is a phone on the nightstand by the bed. You dial the operator. "I need a doctor," you tell her. The line crackles with static from the storm. "It's an emergency. Send an ambulance to—" You are about to say "Officer Porter's apartment," but the words freeze in your throat.

You feel a presence in the room and turn slowly. The woman from the Jeep is standing behind you! You glance over at Officer Porter. His eyes are filled with fear. She must be the one who caused his paralysis—and Dr. Colby's!

"I thought you might come here for help," the woman says. "Put down the phone."

The operator's nasal voice comes through the receiver.

"Where do you want the ambulance sent?" she asks impatiently.

"Put down the phone," the woman repeats. "Say nothing, or your fate will be like his!" She gestures toward the paralyzed man on the bed.

If you answer the operator, turn to page 31.

If you hang up the phone, turn to page 82.

"Now what's troubling you, youngster?" Professor Harrison asks as you drive into the dark and quiet village. "Speak up!"

You pause before you answer. Should you trust him? You swallow. "This is the Jeep the two women were driving," you say. "The ones who dropped the rock in the clearing."

The professor speaks quietly to himself. "So it is Aphir."

"Aphir?" you ask. "Do you know who the women were?"

"Aphir is at the root of this. She is a professor of archaeology from Egypt. The girl who left the rock was a student. She did not know its value. Aphir took the Jeep and went off this afternoon to find the burial mound. I presume she was looking for the mate to the Calusa Sacred Rock."

"Edna told me there was another one," you say.

"Yes, but it's not at the mound. One of my associates on the dig, Dr. Colby, actually found the stone Aphir left in the clearing. When it disappeared, he confronted her."

"What happened?"

"She told Colby he would regret his accusation. That she had not taken the stone. And he did regret it. When Colby didn't show up for dinner, I sent one of the students to his tent. He found him lying on his cot. . . ."

"Was he dead?" you ask, horrified.

"No, he was paralyzed. He could neither move nor speak. We had him transported by ambulance to St. Petersburg."

Turn to page 97.

"How did she know that Edna had the other rock in the first place?" you ask.

"It's my fault," Professor Harrison says. "I lectured to my group about Calusa artifacts on Tuesday. Because the Sacred Stones are so rare, I told them that one had been found years ago by a friend of mine—a fisherman who knew Calusa lore like the back of his hand. I also told them that his widow, who lived in this area, still had it."

"Let's go!" you say. "Edna may be in danger. I'll go back to the *Jolly Mac*. You go to the village and get the police!"

You run to the clearing and stop. Parked beside the professor's car is the woman's red Jeep.

"Too late," he says. "I'll go to the *Jolly Mac* with you."

"No," you reply. "You get the police. I'll stall for time when I get to the boat. We can keep the woman from leaving." As you speak you squat down and let the air out of one of the Jeep's tires. The professor grins and gets into his car. By the time he's left the clearing, the Jeep has four very flat tires.

You run down the dock to the houseboat. Loud voices are coming from the cabin.

"Is the other stone worth your life, Mrs. MacDonald?" the woman asks.

"You don't scare me," Edna replies. "If you want the stone, you'll have to find it."

You enter the cabin. The woman is feverishly pulling cushions from the sofa, while Edna sits calmly at the kitchen table, watching.

Turn to page 105.

You walk along without seeing anything but tall grass and tropical shrubs, and are about ready to turn back when your lantern flashes on something ahead. It's high—at least twice as tall as you are—and it seems to be silver. Could it be a bush of some kind? you wonder. You hurry toward it, squinting through the dark, and then stop. It's the most spectacular thing you've ever seen. Hundreds of thousands of shells, piled in layers, with a mother-of-pearl opalescence that catches the light of your lantern and reflects a soft, glimmering sheen. There's no doubt in your mind: You've found the Calusa burial mound.

"Edna!" you yell. "It's here! This way!"

Within minutes she's at your side, and the two of you stand and stare silently at its beauty.

"Let's go now," she says softly. "We'll come back tomorrow."

Turn to page 9.

"Turtles!" Edna repeats.

You've got to stop her before she says too much! "Let's wait till Matthew gets back," you say, tugging at her sleeve.

Edna gives you a disappointing look. "This won't wait," she says. "That pair could be in France in a week. We need to catch them now, while you can identify them."

"Identify who?" Julie asks, looking at you carefully.

Your heart is pounding. There's no way to stop Edna now.

Quickly she tells Julie about your afternoon adventure. You watch Julie's face carefully for some reaction, but there is none.

"The child can identify them," Edna concludes.

Julie reaches for a clipboard, and looks directly at you. "Good," she says. "Give me a description. Start with the man."

You open your mouth, but nothing comes out.

"There's nothing to be afraid of," says Julie, smiling.

You clear your throat. "The man was about six feet tall," you say, "and he was wearing tennis shoes, no socks, and cutoffs."

"Is that all?" Julie asks.

Go on to the next page.

"No. He had on a lime-green striped shirt and sunglasses with orange lenses, and had medium-long brown hair in a sort of fringe, but he was bald on top."

"And the woman?" she asks, staring at you.

You swallow. Should you tell her you can't remember, so she won't know that you recognize her? Then you could tell Matthew when he comes back. But that might be too late! Maybe you should confront Julie right now!

If you lie about the woman, turn to page 12.

If you confront Julie, turn to page 100.

You take a deep breath and line the rocks up side by side, with the gull facing west. You put your right foot on one rock. It feels cool and smooth on your bare sole. You are about to put your left foot in place when you hear a noise.

Startled, you look up. The driver of the Jeep is standing in the doorway. And she's holding a gun! She looks down at the rocks and a slow smile crosses her face.

"You've made it very easy for me," she says in a heavily accented voice. "There were rumors that Mrs. MacDonald had the other one. I was willing to bargain for it, but now I don't have to. This discovery should assure my promotion—and greatly please the officials in my country. American professors seem to win all the international honors. It's time that was changed!"

Step by step she approaches as you stare at the gun. A feeling of nausea sweeps over you. You try to move, but your legs won't respond. Terrified, you lose your balance. Your left foot touches the rock, and you black out.

When Edna and Professor Harrison return to the boat, you are gone. The woman has vanished. The rocks have disappeared. The only clue they have as to what happened is the frightened sea gull perching on the open lid of the chest.

The End

Most people think you and Edna drowned while attempting to take the old boat out into the Gulf. But a few old-timers talk about that summer morning when thousands of gulls turned the sky black, out over the bay. And some wonder if your disappearance could somehow be connected with the legend of the mysterious Gull Rocks—and discuss how the Calusas worshiped the seabird that gave the bay its name. The bay that claimed yet another victim.

The End

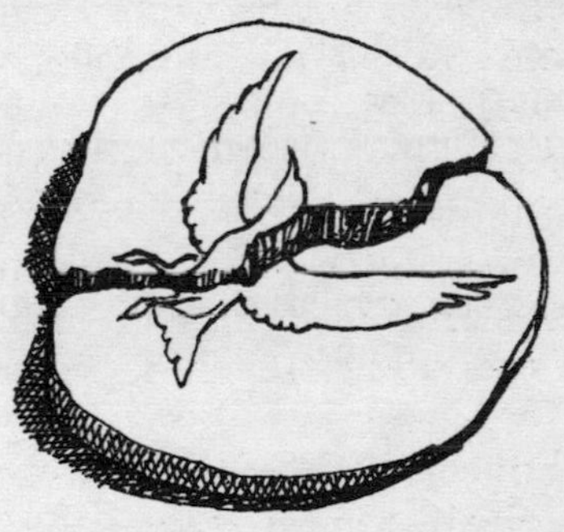

"I'm Roger Randall from Texas," the man says. "I deal in oil and metals."

"So you *are* after the titanium," Edna says angrily. "People like you are a blight! Not only are you stealing, but you're disrupting the ecology. This is a wildlife sanctuary!"

"I'm paid handsomely by foreign countries for providing titanium for their missiles," Randall says. "And I *am* replacing the sand I remove. There's fifty tons of it behind you."

"So that's why this sand is dry," you say. "You take out the titanium-bearing sand and bring in sand from somewhere else. But it's not for the ecology, it's to cover your tracks!"

The man smiles. "You're very perceptive."

"Why were you at Edna's houseboat today?" you demand.

"Mrs. MacDonald is our closest neighbor," he says. "I had to reassure myself that our operation was not visible from her boat. Fortunately for me, it is not. Unfortunately for you, you figured out what I was photographing. That discovery was fatal."

As the man speaks he moves to a set of levers by the railing and pushes one forward. You hear a sucking sound, as though a drain has been opened. Then suddenly you feel your feet slipping from under you as the mountain of sand beside you and Edna shifts. He has opened the chute! Sand swirls around you as it streams out through the bottom of the barge. You reach for the railing, but it is too late. In fifty tons of sand, at the bottom of Alligator Slough, you and Edna are buried.

The End

You race for the boat, jump in, shove off, and row as hard as you can.

Edna is fixing dinner when you get back.

"Well, how was your exploration?" she asks.

"Fine, until I got to the island," you tell her. "Is that private property?"

"Turtle Island? Land sakes, no, child! That's state land. The only private property left around here is mine. Everything else belongs to the State of Florida." She sets some dishes on the table. "Mac and I used to go to Turtle Island every year to watch the green sea turtles coming in to nest. Last time the turtles came was in the late fifties."

"What happened to them?"

"Poachers wiped them out. They butchered the turtles for the eggs and for calipee. They both brought good prices in fancy New York restaurants."

"What's calipee?"

"Calipee is the cartilage over the lower shell. It's used to make turtle soup."

"Yuck," you say. "Well, I didn't see any turtles, but I ran into a bad-tempered man."

"Fishing?" Edna asks.

"No, he and this lady were filling pails," you say.

"With sand?" Edna asks.

"Well, I didn't hang around to get a really good look, but it looked to me as if they were digging up Ping-Pong balls."

"My land," Edna says, taking off her apron. "The turtles must be back! Dinner's on hold. We're going to the village."

Turn to page 45.

"Let's wait till morning," you tell Edna. "I'm hungry."

She looks disappointed, but you're glad that she doesn't press you to change your mind. After dinner Edna makes up a bed for you on the couch in the main cabin area.

"My room's in there," she says, indicating a door that opens off the living room. "The couch is pretty comfortable, or if you want to, you can take the sleeping bag up to the sun deck."

"I think I'll do that," you tell her.

"I'm going to turn in," she says. "I may get up and go fishing in the morning. I'm an early riser."

You say good night and go up to the sun deck. You try to get comfortable, but thoughts of the tourist with the camera keep you awake. Who was he? And why was he on Edna's boat? Finally you get out of the sleeping bag and go to the telescope. You focus it on the area you looked at earlier. A light is visible on the water. A large boat with a powerful headlight is coming out of Alligator Slough.

You hurry down to the cabin and knock on the door to wake Edna.

Turn to page 70.

The professor rummages in the pocket of his jacket. "Here," he says, handing you and Edna each a clam shell. "I took these from the burial mound before Aphir took control of my will. The Calusas wore bracelets and necklaces of shells to ward off evil spirits. The shells might give us some protection."

You slip the shell into your pocket, but you don't really believe it will protect you. You sit down beside Edna. "I wonder what the experiments are going to be," you say.

"It's my guess that she wants to perfect a way to control nature," says Professor Harrison. "Aphir can already control another person's will. If she succeeds in using the Gull Rocks to turn a human being into a bird, then she'll be able to manipulate human life in any evil way she wants."

"Is that what she's going to do?" you ask, wide-eyed. "Turn us into sea gulls?"

As you speak the door opens, and Aphir enters.

"Who will be my first volunteer?" she asks.

Shivers of fear roll up your spine. You feel responsible for this mess you're all in. You should have talked Edna into waiting till morning to go to the mound. Or gotten to her faster when she cried out.

If you volunteer, turn to page 102.

If you don't volunteer, turn to page 44.

You must get the professor! you tell yourself.

You run back into the clearing and stop. Aphir is coming from the dock, straight toward you. Did she find Professor Harrison on the *Jolly Mac*? Is he paralyzed now too? You turn and run back to the mound, but not fast enough. Aphir has seen you.

"You can't escape me!" she calls out.

"What did you do to Edna?" you yell.

Aphir's voice is icy as she steadily approaches. "She is frozen in time. Until I choose to release her, she will remain that way." The slim, dark-haired woman stares coldly at you. "Come here."

"I won't!" you reply heatedly.

"You have no choice," she says. "Come here."

Against your will you walk slowly toward her. You struggle mentally to cast off whatever spell she is working, but your efforts are useless. As you approach there is a shout from the clearing. It's Professor Harrison!

Turn to page 38.

It seems like hours before you hear the sound of a high-powered launch approaching. Is it Albert bringing help? Or is it someone coming to see why the men have been delayed?

A man in a ranger's uniform appears at the top of the stairs.

"Evenin', Mrs. Mac," he says. "Looks like you and your young friend have everything under control here. You should get an award from the department for catching this pair."

Edna grins. "I'd rather get a free fishing license, Matt," she says.

"Well, I'd rather get a free pizza," you say.

"Now, the pizza I can manage," says the ranger, laughing. "Just as soon as I get these two locked up. Let's go!"

The End

"I'll go aboard the barge," you tell Edna.

"All right," she replies. "But be careful. I'll watch for them. If I see anyone coming, I'll whistle once. You come right back to the rowboat."

"Yes, ma'am," you reply as you climb up the metal ladder and drop to the deck of the barge. A railing circles the pile of sand. You walk to one end. To your left is a metal door. You open it cautiously. A stairway!

You descend the stairs and walk down the hall, looking into the rooms: two small bedrooms, an engine room, and a living room–kitchen combination, which you enter. A fancy two-way radio sits on a built-in desk, its green fluorescent dials glowing eerily in the dark room. You beam your lantern ahead of you and walk to the desk. Beside the radio is a clipboard. You direct your light down onto the page. It's a metallurgist's report from a company in Texas, addressed to a Roger Randall. Edna was right! The men are after titanium!

A noise in the hall startles you, and you quickly shut off the lantern and crouch down. It occurs to you that if Edna had whistled, you would not have heard her, down below deck. The door opens.

"Where are you?"

It's Edna!

"Over here, by the desk." You turn on your lantern. "You were right, Edna. They're after the titanium. The guy's name is Roger Randall. Are they coming?"

"Yes," Edna replies. "From the bay side. We have about three minutes. Let me at that radio!" She pushes you aside and turns on the transmitter.

Turn to page 26.

"What is it, child?" Edna asks, coming out of her room.

"There's a boat coming out of Alligator Slough!"

She climbs to the deck to see for herself. "It's a barge," she says. "Riding high and moving fast. Must be self-propelled. I don't see a tugboat." She motions for you to look. "I'm going down to call my friend Albert. He'll get somebody to check on it."

You position yourself at the telescope and keep watch. The barge moves away from the shore toward the open waters of the Gulf. Edna comes back, and the two of you take turns observing.

Turn to page 78.

"I'll go south," you tell Edna.

"All right," she says, "but you be careful. Watch out for quicksand—and snakes! And if you find the mound, be cautious. The Calusa witchcraft is powerful."

You shiver at her warning and gingerly make your way through the shrubbery, holding the lantern high over your head. You've not gone far when you hear Edna cry out.

"Over here! Over here! Come quickly!"

Edna's voice cuts through the stillness of the night, and you run back, taking the path to the north. You squint through the darkness and suddenly stop. Ahead of you is the most magnificent sight you've ever seen: A mound of glimmering opalescent seashells catches the light from your lantern, reflecting it in shimmering waves. The glow from the mound pulsates like a living thing through the dark of the night.

"Edna!" you cry out. "Where are you? Edna?"

But only the sounds of the night reply.

"Edna!"

You work your way carefully around the burial mound, looking for her. Could she have fallen? Or been trapped in a pocket of quicksand? But the ground is solid all the way around the mound, and she's nowhere in sight! Edna has disappeared.

If you go back to the Jolly Mac *and radio for help, turn to page 5.*

If you go to the village to find Professor Harrison, turn to page 87.

Julie turns a spotlight on the island as you approach and swivels it to pan the beach. A shadowy figure starts to run.

"They're still there!" Edna says triumphantly.

They? You look over at her. She has taken a pair of binoculars from her purse and is studying the island. You reach for the binoculars. She's right! There are two people running for the pier. That means Julie is not the woman you saw!

Julie skillfully maneuvers the launch around to the pier and cuts off the couple's access to their motorboat. "Stay here!" she tells you and Edna as she takes out her revolver and climbs up to the wooden platform.

At the sight of the gun the man and woman freeze. You stare in disbelief. The woman could be Julie's double! Julie herds them into the boat and handcuffs them to the rail. "I thought it would be you two," she says with disgust.

Later, when the poachers have been handed over to the local sheriff, Julie explains.

"Eleanor is my cousin," she says. "She went through all the training to be a ranger, but flunked her last exams. She's angry at the state about flunking out, and this is how she gets even. The man is someone she met in New York."

She turns to you. "I had a feeling it was Eleanor when you kept staring at me, and when you wouldn't describe the woman. You thought it was me, didn't you?"

You nod. "I was sure of it," you say. "Seeing is believing!"

"Except with people," says Julie, putting her arm around you.

The End

"Land sakes, you're welcome to take them both, Harry!" Edna says. "Mac said to keep his only until the mate was found."

Professor Harrison shakes his head. "No," he says slowly. "Put it back in the refrigerator. The Calusa wisdom is sound. They must not be kept in the same place. When this one is safely locked up in the university museum, I'll come back for the other."

"Suit yourself," Edna says. "It's been here for over twenty years. A little longer won't bother me. Do you want us to follow you back to the village?"

The professor chuckles. "No," he says. "I'll be quite safe. I may stop on my way out and take a look at the mound."

After he leaves, Edna inspects your work on the pier. "Nice job," she says. "You've earned the afternoon off, and I'm ready for a nap. I don't think our lady friend will be back for a while. Maybe you're ready for a nap too?"

"No way!" you say. "I want to do something exciting!"

Edna rolls her eyes and grins. "As if we haven't had enough excitement," she says. "What did you have in mind?"

Go on to the next page.

"Oh, either go back to the mound or out on the bay," you say.

"The bay's calm today," Edna says, looking out on the water. "Can you handle a rowboat?"

"Yes, my dad taught me last summer."

"Good," she says, covering a yawn with her hand. "You're responsible enough to do either one without me tagging along. I think I can trust you to stay out of trouble."

If you decide to explore Gull Bay, turn to page 21.

If you go back to the burial mound, turn to page 112.

You slide the oars into the water and push away from the barge. It would be foolish to have both of you caught, you tell yourself. This way you will be able to come and get Edna when she whistles the all-clear, or go and get help if too much time passes. You forget about being hungry as you row farther inland. The waterway narrows, and the foliage hangs over the boat like a canopy. You sense things moving in the water by the boat and shiver. The name *Alligator Slough* is not comforting.

Your oar catches on a submerged root. You tighten your grip and press on, occasionally glancing back to see if anyone is following.

Without warning the rowboat strikes something solid and bounces backward. One oar slips from your hand, and you lunge for it as it slides beneath the murky water. You grab the other one with both hands and stand up, trying to use it to retrieve the one that is sinking.

The small boat tips slightly to one side and starts to fill with water. Frantically you step to the other side to right it, but your quick motion only forces more water in. The rowboat sinks quickly. You start to swim toward the bank, but you've taken only a few strokes when what appears to be a dead tree in the water moves quickly toward you.

One beat of the alligator's powerful tail breaks your neck. Edna's disappearance is never solved, but your remains are found in Alligator Slough years later, during a drought.

The End

You track the boat for a long time before another craft comes into view. Then overhead you hear a loud chopping noise, and a searchlight sweeps across the *Jolly Mac* as a helicopter heads toward the barge.

Hours later heavy footsteps on the dock and the off-key whistling of a marching tune that your school band plays announce a visitor.

"That's Albert!" Edna says, hurrying to open the door.

A short man with leathery skin and a gray stubble of beard enters.

Edna introduces you. "Well, you two have had a bit of excitement," he says.

"What were they doing over there?" you ask Albert.

"Taking sand out of Alligator Slough," he replies. "Seems it has a high titanium content."

"But the barge was empty!" Edna says. "It was riding high!"

"Well, they were also bringing sand in," Albert explains, "to replace what they were taking out. They'd just dumped a load. Sure was an exciting evening."

Turn to page 104.

The professor reaches over and touches Edna's arm. "I may have been the cause of your break-in last night," he says apologetically. "I lectured on the Gull Rocks two days ago. I said a friend of mine had found one, and as far as I knew, it was still with his widow. I was going to ask you to lend it to me so I could show them."

"Well, there are *two* in the area now," Edna says crisply, "and we have to get rid of one of them."

"I agree," says the professor. He rewraps the rock in the newspapers. "My student assistant is leaving this morning for Miami. I'll have him take this to the university for safekeeping. We'll talk later about what to do with the other one."

You and Edna don't talk much on the way back to the *Jolly Mac.* You really don't believe in the power of the rocks, but she and the professor seem to. And so does the woman thief!

"Let's have a snack before we start work," Edna says.

Turn to page 16.

Edna points to the Gull Rock lying between your feet. It is shattered into a dozen pieces.

"But she was aiming at my head!" you say. "And we were within firing range. Where's the bullet? Did it go through the boat? Are we taking in water?"

"No, child," Edna says calmly. "The bullet is not here, and there's no hole in the boat."

Piece by piece she starts dropping the remains of the Sacred Stone into the bay. "The Sacred Rock has done its work. Thanks to its power you are alive."

"But how?" you ask.

Edna shrugs. "How does magic work?" she asks. "If we knew, it wouldn't be magic." She looks back at the pier. "Harry and the police have the woman in custody. We can go back."

You follow her gaze to the dock and see a policeman leading the woman away. Professor Harrison is standing on the pier, waiting for you to return.

You pick up the last piece of the Sacred Stone and hold it in your hand, looking at it. Finally you raise your arm and throw, watching as the stone arcs out over the glistening water and drops, cutting the surface cleanly as it disappears.

You smile at Edna and turn the boat around, heading back for the *Jolly Mac*.

The End

You hang up the receiver. The sound of the storm outside adds to your anxiety.

"Very good," says the woman. "Now we will join the others."

What others? you wonder. A warm feeling surges through your body, and you feel weightless and detached. You hear Edna's voice.

"I'm sorry, child. I hoped you'd escape her."

Edna is seated on a stone bench in a small bare room. She is holding your hand. "I thought you would go and get Harry."

"I did," you whisper. "But I thought he was one of them. He was driving the red Jeep. Who is she? Where are we?"

"I don't now," Edna says. As she speaks the door opens, and Professor Harrison enters. The woman is behind him.

"Make yourselves comfortable," she says. "I'll let you rest for a while before we start the experiments." She leaves, closing the door behind her.

"I'm sorry I didn't trust you," you say to Professor Harrison. "But you were driving the same Jeep she had at the clearing."

He pats your shoulder. "That's all right," he says. "You had a choice to make. In the long run it may have been the best one. We rarely know ahead of time, and sometimes never."

"Who is she?" you ask him.

"Her name is Aphir," he replies. "She is a professor of archaeology from Egypt who requested to work at our dig. But I believe she is also an Evil Ancient."

"What's that?" you ask.

Turn to page 4.

The professor turns to look at you. "Edna's husband, Mac, found the mate to a Gull Rock years ago, at a Calusa burial site about twenty miles from here. I believe it may match the one Colby found. Edna kept it in a small chest on the *Jolly Mac.*"

"What are we going to do?" you ask him.

"We have two things to do," says the professor. "One of us has to go to the *Jolly Mac* and get the stones. The other must go to the burial mound and find Edna—and keep Aphir from any further destruction. Unfortunately we may be too late on both counts. Which do you want to do?"

If you decide to go to the Jolly Mac,
turn to page 20.

*If you go to the burial mound,
turn to page 89.*

You look at Professor Harrison and nod your head. Then you sit down and tell him what happened.

"Hurry!" he says when you are finished. "Edna is in grave danger. I'll tell you the story of the rock on the way. It is a rare and powerful artifact."

Rain pounds down, and thunder growls overhead as he leads you to a compound where several vehicles are parked.

"Get in!" he says impatiently. But for a moment you stand rooted to the spot. The vehicle he's getting into is the red Jeep the women were driving! No license plate. Scratch on the side. Hesitantly you climb in. The engine roars to life, and the professor pulls out on to the road.

You're not convinced of Professor Harrison's story about a dream. Does he really want to help? Or is he involved in Edna's disappearance? He knew about the burial mound, and the rock. If you go to the mound with him, you may disappear too. But if you don't go, what will happen to Edna? Maybe you should go only as far as the village and get the police.

Turn to page 90.

Early the next morning Edna starts out for the village. When her green pickup has disappeared from view, you head for the burial mound.

The hill of shells is still impressive, but the eeriness that you felt last night is gone. In the early-morning sun you feel more curiosity than fear. Slowly you circle the mound, looking for other artifacts that might be valuable, but your search is futile.

You decide to explore the area, and push through the tall marsh grass, stopping now and then to inspect a tropical plant or stare back at a curious bird.

You've traveled about half a mile when you notice the ground is getting soggier. Soon you are at the edge of a small pond. On the other side is a circular building, like a park bandstand, its wooden frame bleached white-gray by the weather.

You wonder what purpose it might have had out here, for there is no other sign of civilization. At first you try to approach it from the left, but the vegetation growing out of the swamp offers no firm footing, and you sink almost to your knees in thick muck. Pushing aside the dense foliage, you go back to the right, and are about to give up when you uncover the overturned shell of a canoe.

Turn to page 94.

You look carefully for Edna one more time before you start jogging to the village. A strong wind has come up, and you struggle to maintain your pace as you face into it. Sheet lightning flashes across the sky. You think about Edna's warning: "The Calusa witchcraft is powerful!"

Does she really believe in witchcraft? you wonder skeptically. You don't. But her sudden disappearance has made you nervous.

Rain plasters your hair to your forehead as you move down the deserted main street of the village. Edna said the dig site was east of town. Half a mile down the road you see a cluster of tents just outside a large area that has been roped off.

A light trickles through the open flap of one of the tents, and a short white-haired man appears in the doorway.

"Professor Harrison?" you whisper.

"Yes, I'm Harry Harrison," he says. "Come in. I've been expecting you." He hands you a towel.

"Expecting me?" you say in surprise.

He puts his fingers to his lips and motions you inside. "Mac came to me in a dream," he whispers. "He told me Edna was in trouble and that someone would bring me news."

You start backing out of the tent. Is he crazy? you ask yourself.

"No, please wait!" he says, grabbing your arm. "It frightens me too. But I did dream it! I wakened about an hour ago. And there was a Calusa burial mound. And the Gull Rocks. Is that why you're here?"

Turn to page 84.

"I feel responsible for Edna," you tell the professor. "I'll go back to the burial mound."

"Take the lantern," he says, pulling into the clearing. "I'll join you as soon as I get the rocks from the *Jolly Mac.*"

You jump out and start walking. Your heart begins pounding as you approach the shimmering glow of the mound. You circle it silently, looking for Edna. You hear a faint noise and look up. Hovering over the top of the pile of shells is a lone sea gull. You turn once again to the task of finding Edna in the tall, sharp saw grass. You're almost back at your starting point when you trip over a mangrove root. You reach out to break your fall, and your hand hits something that feels like canvas. A shoe! Hastily you pull aside the grass. It's Edna! She's alive, but lying motionless on the swampy ground, her eyes staring straight up.

Turn to page 66.

"Let me tell you about the Calusas," the professor says. "They worshiped nature. They believed that rocks from the earth, birds of the air, and shells from the sea had special powers. That is why the Gull Stone was sacred to the Calusa tribe. They believed it had such great power that when the shaman finished the etching, he took a stone mallet and broke the rock in two so the power would be divided. Matching stones were never kept in the same camp."

"Why not?" you ask. "What power do they have?"

He leans over. "The Calusas believed that any person stepping on the stones would be transformed into a gull!"

If you decide to go with Professor Harrison, turn to page 52.

If you decide to go to the police, turn to page 109.

Neither you nor Edna sleep well, and at dawn you're on your way to see Professor Harrison at the dig site. The rock, carefully wrapped in newspapers, is stashed under the seat of the truck.

When you arrive, Professor Harrison ushers the two of you into his tent. Once inside, Edna hands him the package and explains why you've come. His hands tremble as he unwraps the rock.

"You still have the mate?" he asks, looking at Edna.

She nods. "Yes, that's why I wanted to get rid of this one."

"You mean, you have both of them?" you ask.

Edna turns to you. "Yes, Mac found the other Sacred Stone years ago at a burial mound a hundred miles from here."

Turn to page 79.

"Mac found the mate years ago, at a burial mound twenty miles from here. He said I was never to part with it until the other half was found." Her eyes drift over to a small wooden chest in the corner. "He was sure the other half was here at Gull Bay—and he was right."

"What kind of power does it have?" you ask skeptically.

"When placed side by side with its mate, with the gull facing west," Edna says, "it will transform any person who puts one foot on each rock into its image."

"Into a gull?" you ask, trying to keep from laughing.

Edna nods. "The Sacred Stones are said to have such power that after the shaman finished the etching, he would take a stone mallet and break the rock in two, so the power would be divided. Matching stones were never kept in the same camp. That's why no one has ever found a set at one site."

"Can I see the other stone?" you ask.

Go on to the next page.

"No!" she snaps. "You're not to touch either stone until I've talked to Professor Harrison at the dig site east of the village." She takes the rock and puts it back in the refrigerator. "Catch some shut-eye, child. I'll get Harry Harrison in the morning."

You roll back into bed, but you can't sleep. Your eyes keep moving to the carved chest in the corner. Is the mate for the Sacred Stones in there? you ask yourself. Are there other treasures at the burial mound? Should you look in the chest while Edna's in the village? Or go back to the mound when she leaves?

If you decide to look in the chest,
turn to page 24.

If you choose to go back to the mound,
turn to page 86.

Excited by your find, you examine the boat. It looks seaworthy, but there's only one way to be sure. You figure that if you raise one end off the ground and look through the hull from the inside, any sunlight coming through will quickly point out holes and cracks.

You raise one end until it's above your head and shoulders, then duck underneath to examine the frame. It's dark, and the musty smell inside catches at your throat, but no light leaks through!

You are about to roll the boat over to rest on its base, when you feel a sharp sting on your neck. You drop the end you're holding and slap your hand to the side of your throat. As you do an ugly multilegged creature drops to the boat's rim and crawls slowly away. A scorpion!

You've been bitten by a scorpion!

You turn and thrash through the grass, heading back toward the clearing and the *Jolly Mac.* But the venom travels faster than you do. Your run is slowed to a walk, and then to a crawl.

You try to call for help, but your throat is closing. You can't breathe; you can't speak. You get only as far as the edge of the burial mound—a fitting place for your body to be found.

The End

You reach for the ladder on the side of the barge. You can't leave Edna alone up there!

"Edna!" you whisper, as you drop to the deck. "Where are you?" A waist-high railing marks off a square around the immense mountain of sand.

"I'm over here," she replies crossly. "Why didn't you stick with the boat and get it out of sight, like you were supposed to?"

You climb over the railing to where she is crouching by the pile of sand.

"I couldn't leave you alone," you say. "Where are they?"

"Coming in from the northwest," she whispers. "They've dredged a new waterway through the mangrove forest."

"They must be coming to take out the sand," you say.

"I think they're bringing it in," she replies. "Look, this is all dry." She lets a handful trickle through her fingers. "If this were what they dredged up, it would be wet, and packed solid."

"But why would they bring sand in?" you ask.

Your question is interrupted by voices.

"Someone came in that rowboat, Randall," a man says. "And whoever it is, is still on the barge."

You hear two thumps on the deck, and you know the men have boarded.

"Ah-ha!" says a sarcastic voice above you. "Mrs. MacDonald and her young friend are here, Jake."

You look up to face the man who was taking pictures from the sun deck of the *Jolly Mac.*

Turn to page 60.

"Did Aphir poison Dr. Colby?" you ask Professor Harrison.

"In a manner of speaking," he replies. "I believe she cast a spell on him."

"A spell?" you shout. "Like in a fairy tale? You're kidding!"

"I believe Aphir is one of the evil ancients," he continues, ignoring your outburst. "A person so thoroughly wicked that no time frame will claim her. She floats back and forth through the centuries, causing destruction to satisfy her own wants. Only nature's force can stop an evil ancient."

He speaks so seriously, you're beginning to believe him. "Nature's force?" you ask.

"Earth, wind, fire, or water," he replies grimly. "I tried to question Colby about the rock, but he couldn't speak. His vocal cords had been paralyzed along with the rest of his body."

"Why is the rock so important?" you ask.

"Because no one in modern times has ever possessed a matching pair before."

"What do you mean, *before*?" you ask.

Turn to page 83.

"Didn't you ever look for the burial mound before?" you ask.

"My lands, yes!" Edna replies. "Mac and I went over this property inch by inch, many times."

"Then why are we looking tonight?" you ask, puzzled.

Edna grins at you. "Florida land is slippery, child. It's alive. It moves. Sometimes, a few years after folks build a house, they have to add an extra step to the porch, 'cause the house is raised six inches. And sometimes whole lakes just disappear overnight—like somebody pulled the plug in a bathtub. Fortunately we've got a lot of lakes. So you see, the burial mound could have been here all along, but until the time was right, we wouldn't have found it." She stops walking.

Overhead the moon is shining silver on the tall grass. Ahead you can see two paths where the grass has been beaten down.

"We'll be here till midnight checking both paths," Edna says with a frown. "Guess we'll have to wait till morning."

"No, we won't!" you say. "You go one way, I'll go the other."

She looks at you questioningly. "Aren't you afraid?"

"A little," you say. "But I want to go on."

"Okay," says Edna. "Which path do you want?"

If you take the path to the North,
turn to page 49.

If you take the path to the South,
turn to page 71.

"What did the woman look like?" Julie asks.

"You," you say. "She looked exactly like you."

"Are you accusing the ranger of poaching?" Edna asks.

Julie gestures at Edna. "It's all right," she says.

You look at her warily. Is she being nice to make you less suspicious?

"I know what you're thinking," Julie says. "You'll have proof shortly that the woman you saw was not me." She picks up the phone and dials a number. "Captain Long, please," she says. There is a short pause. "Ed, Eleanor's back in the area. . . . Yes, Turtle Island. There's a man with her. Will you have someone pick them up? I have an eyewitness."

Later, after you've picked the poachers out of a lineup at the local police station, Julie explains.

"Eleanor is my cousin," she says. "She flunked out of ranger training and has been getting even with the state ever since. She knew the state was working with a conservation group to get the turtles back to the island, so she took advantage of that knowledge for personal gain."

"You look like twins!" you say.

"Our mothers were twins," Julie explains. "We've been mistaken for each other before. It took courage for you to be that honest with me." She smiles at you. "In a way you're like the turtles you saved today."

"What do you mean?" you ask, puzzled.

"A turtle never gets anywhere," Julie tells you, "until it sticks its neck out."

The End

The oars dip softly into the water, and the boat glides away. You raise your arm high and send the board spinning, end over end. But your aim is not accurate. The board hits the water with a splat, and the woman escapes in the vast expanse of the bay.

"What's going on out here, child?" Edna asks, from behind you, clutching an old bathrobe around her.

"The woman driving the Jeep came back and stole the rock," you say, puzzled.

"I suspected she'd try," Edna says, "but I didn't think she'd come back tonight. I'm sorry. It must have been frightening."

"I don't get it. What's so special about the rock?"

"Come inside. I'll tell you."

You follow her into the cabin and watch as she goes to the refrigerator. To your surprise she takes the rock from a shelf and hands it to you.

"But I saw her pick it up! It was on the sink!"

"That was a rock I use for a doorstop," Edna says. "I put this one in the refrigerator before I went to bed."

"Why?" you ask.

"This rock has special powers." She takes it from you and traces her finger along the etching of the bird. "The Calusa Indians had strange rituals and beliefs. This rock is one of their sacred artifacts. Coupled with its mate, it has great power. To my knowledge no one has ever had a matched set before."

"Before," you repeat. "Do you have the mate?"

Edna nods. "Yes," she says. "I do."

Turn to page 92.

"I'll volunteer," you say to Aphir.

Professor Harrison protests, but Aphir brushes him aside and pushes you into the hallway, closing the door firmly behind you. Your fingers curl tightly around the clam shell in your pocket.

You follow her down the hall to a glass-enclosed room that looks like a greenhouse. Strange plants fill the large area. On your left is a pine tree bearing strawberries, and in front of you is a giant cactus from which misshapen ferns are growing.

"My creations are unique," Aphir says proudly. "I can produce things that nature cannot."

You look around you fearfully, trying to find an escape route. Rain washes down the glass walls and roof of the room, and you can hear the whine of the wind. Aphir's eyes dart up to the ceiling as a yellow flash of lightning crosses the sky. Then she walks quickly to a long table by one of the glass walls. In front of the table, on the floor, a triangle of plants has been arranged. On the table are the Calusa Gull Rocks—the pair, perfectly matched. She hands you one of the rocks and, holding the other, moves into the triangle.

"Come," she says, setting her rock on the floor at the tip of the triangle. "You, too, will become one of my creations."

She's mad, you think. Utterly c-r-a-z-y! You back away.

"Come!" she repeats impatiently.

Your heart pounds. You're not going to be her next experiment, you tell yourself. You must escape! You look at the rock in your hand.

Turn to page 35.

"I don't understand it," says the driver to his partner. "This is just like the university fellow over at the dig site. At least he was still alive when we picked him up."

"No sign of foul play," says the attendant.

"It's spooky," says the driver, throwing a sheet over you. "Like an evil presence or something. A curse."

His partner looks at him and frowns. "Don't tell me you believe in that nonsense," he says. "There's a medical reason. The lab will track it down. Maybe a virus or something."

From behind the drapes where she has concealed herself the evil woman smiles. Her next stop is the burial mound. Her next victim—Professor Harrison.

The End

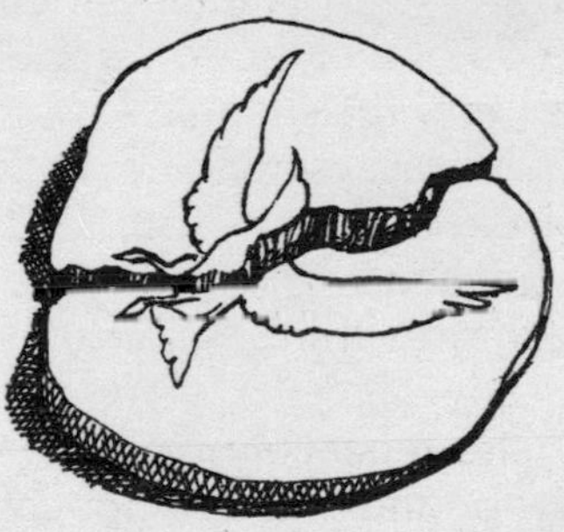

Albert puts his empty cup down on the counter. "Thanks for the coffee. I'll be on my way. Just thought I'd better check to see that you were all right," he says to Edna.

"And why wouldn't I be all right?" Edna asks indignantly.

Albert grins. "Just seems out of character for you to find that fellow here and suspect that something was happening, and not go and check it out for yourself. I thought you might be sick."

"That was my fault," you say sheepishly. "I talked her into waiting till morning. I was hungry—and it's out of character for me to ignore my stomach!"

The End

"I put the rock in the professor's car, like you told me," you say to Edna as you enter. You speak loudly, ignoring the woman. "He must still be at the mound. I didn't see him around."

The woman stops her frantic search and whirls around to face you. Edna look at you quizzically and nods.

"Oh," you say, pretending innocence. "I didn't know you had company."

"In the professor's car?" she repeats. She pushes you out of the way and starts out the door.

"Quick!" you whisper to Edna. You hear the woman's footsteps pounding on the dock as she runs to the clearing. "Untie the rowboat and get in! I'll be right there!"

Edna hurries out to the boat, and you wrench open the refrigerator door and grab the stone. You run to the boat and climb in. Edna quickly pushes off, then you row as hard as you can. The woman has already discovered that the professor's car is gone and is running back toward the *Jolly Mac.*

You row feverishly, but it feels as if the boat is stuck. It won't move! The woman raises the weapon and points it directly at your head. Edna ducks down as low as she can. You hear the crack of the gun and wonder why you don't feel any pain. Suddenly the boat starts moving! With each stroke it goes farther and farther out into the bay. You can't believe you're still alive!

"It must have been a misfire," you say to Edna, your voice choking with fear.

"No," she replies softly. "It was Calusa magic."

Turn to page 81.

You open your mouth to scream, but no sound comes out. Are your vocal cords paralyzed? you ask yourself. The flame from the lantern pulsates as you struggle to gain control. Flame! The professor said a natural force would stop her! Your arm is leaden as you lift it slowly, mustering all your will for that one act. With a strangled cry you hurl the rock at the lantern.

The sound of shattering glass breaks the spell, and you leap up just as Aphir flings herself at you, scratching and clawing. Out of the corner of your eye you see the curtains ignite, then the old wooden drainboard. The boat is on fire! On the floor you tussle with Aphir, choking and gasping as smoke fills the small area, and flames lick down the sides of the cabinet.

Aphir is strong. You can't get out of her grasp. The cabin is in flames, and you roll toward the door, struggling to free yourself, feeling the heat on your feet as the flames lick against your ankles. Suddenly Aphir's viselike grip loosens. She seems to be losing strength. Her fingers clutching your arm slip aside, as if they were only pieces of rubber. She has given up the fight! You crawl out the door, reaching back through the smoke for her arm to draw her away from the flames. But Aphir has disappeared!

Run! your mind commands, and your blistered legs obey. Hurting with every stride, you run the length of the pier and collapse in a heap in the clearing as flames leap up from the doomed houseboat.

Turn to page 114.

You get out of bed quietly and creep to Edna's bedroom door, knocking once before you enter.

"Edna!" you whisper. "Wake up! The woman from the Jeep came back. She stole the rock!"

Edna sits up quickly when you speak.

"I thought that might happen," she says, getting out of bed.

She bustles out to the kitchen and opens the refrigerator. "This is the real rock," she says, handing it to you. "The one she took is one I use for a doorstop."

"I don't get it," you say. "Why is the rock so valuable?"

"It's a Calusa Sacred Stone," Edna replies. "Coupled with its mate, it has great power."

"What kind of power?" you ask apprehensively.

She takes the rock from you and places it carefully on the floor. "The Calusas believed that when its mate was placed beside it with the gull facing west, it would transform any person who puts one foot on each rock into its image."

"Into a gull?" you ask, trying not to laugh.

Edna nods seriously. "Yes, that's why it's broken. To divide its power. When the shaman finished the etching, he broke the rock in two with a stone mallet. Matching stones were never kept in the same camp."

She pushes a chair up against the door to secure it. "Try to get some sleep," she says. "In the morning we'll take the rock to Professor Harrison in the village."

Turn to page 91.

"Professor," you say, "I don't think we can handle this ourselves. I want to go to the police."

"As you wish," he says, much to your surprise. "Officer Porter lives in an apartment up over the grocery store. It's just a block from here." In a few minutes he pulls over to the curb and points to a brick building. "Go up those wooden stairs. I'll go on and look for Edna." He turns to face you. "But I must warn you. We are dealing with supernatural forces. Tonight one of my colleagues was struck with a mysterious paralysis. He was taken to the hospital in St. Petersburg. Dr. Colby knew about the Sacred Stones."

You look at him. What's with this professor? Is he lying? Trying to scare you off?

"I must report Edna's disappearance," you say, getting out.

Without another word he drives off, leaving you on the dark, rain-slicked street. Quickly you climb the rickety stairs to Officer Porter's apartment. A sliver of light shows under the ill-fitting door. Your knock echoes eerily. Nervously you look behind you before you knock again. There is no response. You put your hand on the knob and turn it. The door is unlocked. You enter the sparsely furnished living room. A lamp is lit by an easy chair, and a magazine lies on the floor. Another door, slightly open, is ahead of you. You walk across the room and enter Officer Porter's bedroom. He is lying on the bed, still in uniform, his holstered gun at his side. His eyes are open, but he does not seem to see you. Is he dead? you wonder.

Turn to page 51.

110

You've gone only a couple of miles when the announcer breaks into the music program you're listening to on the truck radio.

"We interrupt this program for a special news bulletin. A fishing vessel has reported seeing a small white seaplane go down in the Gulf. Observers on the boat said the plane's engines were audible and functioning at the time of the accident. They compared the plane to a gull soaring in sweeping curves and finally diving into the water. No flight plan had been filed. The F.A.A. is investigating."

"Together the rocks had great power," Edna says, looking at you. "I'm glad they're gone."

And, after hearing that special bulletin, you're glad too!

The End

"Why were you taking pictures from my boat?" Edna demands.

"You're our closest neighbor, Mrs. MacDonald," Randall says. "I had to be sure that you couldn't observe our equipment or activities from your sun deck." He pauses to smile at her. "By the way, we picked up your cute little message to your friend Albert. You realize, of course, that a small boat—or even two—will not stop the barge."

Edna's face pales. "You won't get away with it," she says. "Albert will bring Matthew with him. He's the state ranger. He'll be armed."

"Thanks for warning me," Randall says, taking a small revolver from his jacket. "Then I'll have to take you up on deck to act as my shield."

"Even if you kill us out there on the Gulf, you'll get caught," you say. "They'll radio ahead and intercept the barge."

"Dumb kid," Randall replies. "When we rid ourselves of you and Mrs. MacDonald, we'll be boarding a submarine. The barge will be scuttled!" He grabs Edna's arm. "Now, move!"

You know where the engine room is located. Is Jake still in there? you wonder. Should you make a run for it and try to shut down the equipment, or go up on deck with Edna? Randall doesn't seem to think you're a threat. He's almost ignoring you!

If you run for the engine room,
turn to page 28.

If you go up on deck with Edna,
turn to page 41.

"I think I'll go back to the burial mound," you tell Edna. "I'd like to see it in daylight."

"Be back by sundown," she cautions you.

As you leave the *Jolly Mac* the glint of the sun on something shiny catches your attention. It's the woman's knife. You pick it up and carefully slip it in your belt. You notice that the professor's car is still in the clearing, and you call out to him as you hurry along the trail to the sacred site.

"Professor!" you yell again as the mound comes into view. "Professor Harrison!" But there is no reply.

You stand very still, listening. Your sixth sense tells you that something is wrong.

A faint gurgling sound comes from the far side of the mound, and you circle around cautiously. The professor, bound and gagged, is lying on the ground. Blood trickles from the side of his head, but his eyes are focused on you. Quickly you remove the gag from his mouth and, using the woman's knife, cut the ropes from his wrists and ankles.

"Who did this?" you ask.

"One of my own people," he replies angrily. "A visiting professor from Egypt who is a guest on the dig!"

"The woman from the Jeep?" you ask.

The professor nods. "She's got the Gull Rock that Edna gave me," he says. "And it's my guess that now that she knows the first rock she took was a fake, she'll stash the Gull Rock, then go back to the *Jolly Mac* to get the other."

Turn to page 53.

The next day Edna and the professor come to visit you in the hospital where you are being treated for second-degree burns on both legs.

"Edna!" you say. "The professor found you!"

Edna grins. "You almost did too," she says. "When you came to the mound after I called out, you were within inches of me. I could have reached through the marsh grass and grabbed your ankle, but I couldn't move or talk."

"Aphir had paralyzed you?"

"Yes, like Dr. Colby."

"I tried to save her," you say, turning your head into the pillow. "I reached back into the cabin for her, but I couldn't see her for the smoke. It was as if she'd evaporated."

Professor Harrison pats your arm. "Don't feel guilty," he says. "You couldn't have saved her. She did evaporate—and good riddance. That released Dr. Colby and Edna from her spell."

"What about the Gull Rocks?" you ask. "And the *Jolly Mac*?"

"By now the rocks are somewhere out in the Gulf," says Edna. "And it's just as well. As for the *Jolly Mac,* it's fully insured, thank goodness. It can be replaced. We'll go houseboat shopping as soon as the doctor releases you."

"Then I can stay through the summer?" you ask.

"If you want to," says Edna. "The dock needs a lot of work after the fire. But repairing it will be a boring job."

"*Boring* will be fine for a while!" you reply.

The End

Don't tempt fate! you tell yourself.

You put one rock in the refrigerator and the other in the chest, taking care to put things back just as you found them.

You're walking back to your job on the pier, when you notice something glimmering in one of the pilings. It's the woman's knife. Edna hustled you into the cabin so quickly last night, you forgot about it. You pull it out and stare at the blade before laying it down on the slats beside you.

You go back to your scraping. The sun is hot, and your arm and shoulder are getting tired. You work a long time before you hear Edna's truck pull into the clearing. A Volkswagen follows her, and a man climbs out. That must be Professor Harrison, you tell yourself. You hurry to meet them.

Edna introduces you, and you all go inside.

"Here you are, Harry," she says, taking the rock from the refrigerator.

The professor examines the etching on the rock. "Magnificent!" he says. His voice drops. "You still have the other?"

Edna nods, and your heart skips a beat as she lifts the lid of the chest. Will she be able to tell that you've been snooping? you wonder. She gives no sign as she pulls out the mate and hands it to the professor.

He lines the rocks up side by side, stares at them for a long time, and then picks one up. "May I take this one back to the dig with me? There's a vault there. It will be safe until I can get it back to the university."

Turn to page 74.

Wave after wave of gulls close in on Aphir. She backs up, trips, and falls. Then, with choreographed precision, each bird swoops down to the burial mound, picks up one shell, and drops it on the spot where Aphir has fallen. They are moving the mound!

Within minutes the ten-foot-high heap of glimmering opalescent shells has become Aphir's burial mound—moved six feet west of its original position, but otherwise unchanged.

Later, when you've rescued the professor and you're all safely back on the houseboat, you ask him why you didn't turn into a gull.

"Many tribes believed that when their sacred artifacts were used for personal gain, the power would be turned against the user. That's why the gulls saved you and destroyed Aphir."

As he speaks you hear a tapping at the cabin window. You look up. A lone gull stares back at you through the glass.

The End

"Come, child," Edna says. "It's all over now."

You open your eyes. You are lying on the ground by the burial mound. Professor Harrison helps you to your feet.

"Aphir?" you ask, looking around apprehensively.

"She is gone," says the professor. "Trapped in her own world of evil. She won't return. Her power over humans is finished."

"Come," Edna repeats. "We'll go back to the *Jolly Mac.*"

You turn for one last look at the burial mound. In the light of dawn you can see a few gulls circling over its shimmering shape.

"What is it, child?" Edna asks.

"The Calusas were right," you say. "Rocks from the earth, birds of the air, and shells from the sea have special powers for both good and evil."

You open your hand to reveal the clam shell. "This belongs here."

You raise your arm and place the shell carefully on the mound. Then, without a backward glance, you walk toward the clearing and the *Jolly Mac.*

The End

ABOUT THE AUTHOR

LOUISE MUNRO FOLEY is the author of many books for younger readers, including *The Lost Tribe, Danger at Anchor Mine,* and *Forest of Fear, Mystery of the Sacred Stones,* in the Choose Your Own Adventure series. She has also written a newspaper column, and her articles have appeared in the *Christian Science Monitor, The Horn Book,* and *Writer's Digest.* Ms. Foley has won several national awards for writing and editing. In addition to writing, she has hosted shows on radio and television in the United States and Canada. A native of Toronto, Ontario, Canada, Ms. Foley now lives in Sacramento, California. She has two sons.

ABOUT THE ILLUSTRATOR

LESLIE MORRILL is a designer and illustrator whose work has won him numerous awards. He has illustrated over thirty books for children, including the Bantam Classics edition of *The Wind in the Willows;* and for the Choose Your Own Adventure series, *Lost on the Amazon, Mountain Survival, Danger at Anchor Mine, The Brilliant Dr. Wogan,* and *Journey to the Year 3000* and *Danger Zones,* Bantam Super Adventures. His work has also appeared frequently in *Cricket* magazine. A graduate of the Boston Museum School of Fine Arts, Mr. Morrill lives near Boston, Massachusetts.